AR 0.9
0.5 pt

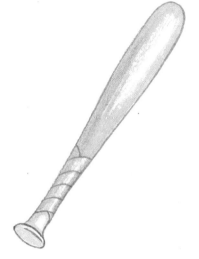

For Peter and Laura
—A.S.C.

For Alyssa,
for all the wonderful stories
that let me do what I do
—P.S.

I Can Read Book® is a trademark of HarperCollins Publishers.

Biscuit Plays Ball
Text copyright © 2012 by Alyssa Satin Capucilli
Illustrations copyright © 2012 by Pat Schories
All rights reserved. Printed in the United States of America. No part of this book may be used or reproduced in any manner whatsoever without written permission except in the case of brief quotations embodied in critical articles and reviews. For information address HarperCollins Children's Books, a division of HarperCollins Publishers, 10 East 53rd Street, New York, NY 10022.
www.icanread.com

Library of Congress Cataloging-in-Publication Data is available.
ISBN 978-0-06-193503-9 (trade bdg.) — ISBN 978-0-06-193502-2 (pbk.)

12 13 14 15 16 LP/WOR 10 9 8 7 6 5 4 3 2   ❖   First Edition

I Can Read!™

Biscuit Plays Ball

story by ALYSSA SATIN CAPUCILLI
pictures by PAT SCHORIES

HARPER
An imprint of HarperCollinsPublishers

It's time to play ball, Biscuit.

Woof, woof!

Look, Biscuit.

The game is about to begin.

Woof, woof!

Stay here now, Biscuit.

You can watch.

Woof, woof!

Wait, Biscuit.

Where are you going?

Woof!

You can't play ball now, Biscuit.

There are no dogs
in this ball game.

Stay here, Biscuit.

Woof, woof!

Uh-oh, Biscuit.

Not again!

Woof, woof!

Come along, Biscuit.
There are no dogs
in this ball game.

Won't you stay here, Biscuit?

Woof, woof!

Biscuit does not want to stay.

Woof, woof!

Biscuit wants to play, too.

Woof!

Biscuit wants to run.

Woof!

Biscuit wants to jump.

Woof!

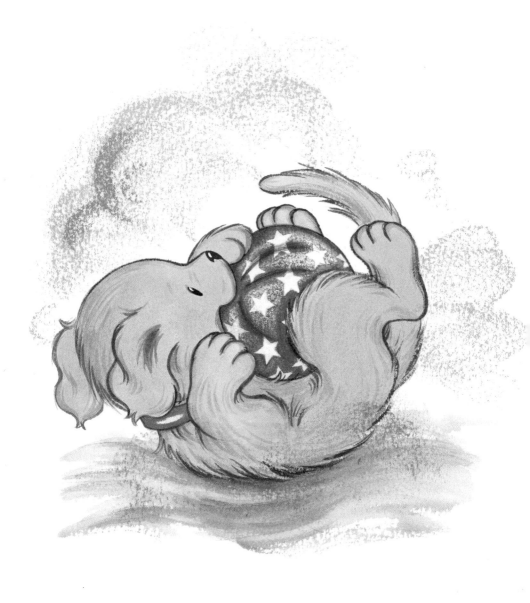

Biscuit wants to play ball!

Woof, woof!

Oh no, Biscuit.

Come back with the ball!

Silly puppy.

How can we play now?

Woof, woof! Woof, woof!

Bow wow!

Oh, Biscuit!

You found your friend Puddles.

Time for all of us!
Woof!

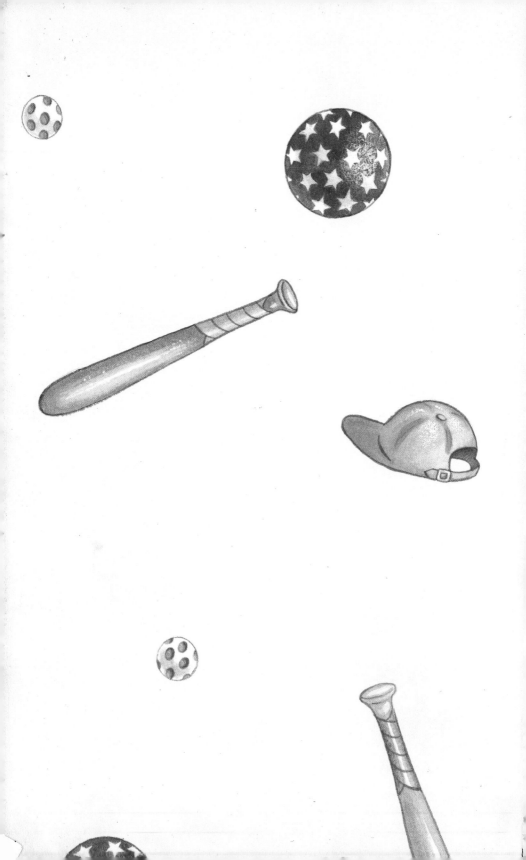